Where's the Baby?

by PAT HUTCHINS

RED FOX

OTHER PICTURE BOOKS BY PAT HUTCHINS

Changes, Changes · Clocks and More Clocks

Don't Forget the Bacon! · The Doorbell Rang · Good-Night, Owl!

Happy Birthday, Sam · King Henry's Palace

One-Eyed Jake · 1 Hunter

Rosie's Walk · The Silver Christmas Tree

The Surprise Party · Titch

The Very Worst Monster · Tom and Sam

The Wind Blew

(Winner of the Kate Greenaway Medal for 1974)

You'll Soon Grow Into Them, Titch · Tidy Titch

A Red Fox Book

Published by Random Century Children's Books
20 Vauxhall Bridge Road, London SW1V 2SA

A division of the Random Century Group
London Melbourne Sydney Auckland
Johannesburg and agencies throughout the world

First published by The Bodley Head 1988
This edition Red Fox 1992

Copyright © Pat Hutchins 1988

Printed in Hong Kong

ISBN 0 09 919621 2

FOR OUR KELLY

"Where's the baby?" Grandma cried.

"In the garden," Ma replied.

"Making a mess," said Hazel.

"Oh dear!" Ma shouted in alarm,
grabbing hold of Grandma's arm.
"He's gone!"

But Hazel noticed on the floor
footprints in the corridor.
"They lead to the kitchen,"
                    Hazel cried,

and everybody rushed inside.

The mixture for the chocolate cake,
that Ma was just about to bake,
was tipped on the table and spilled on the floor.
There were sticky fingerprints on the door.
"He's a help in the kitchen," said Grandma.

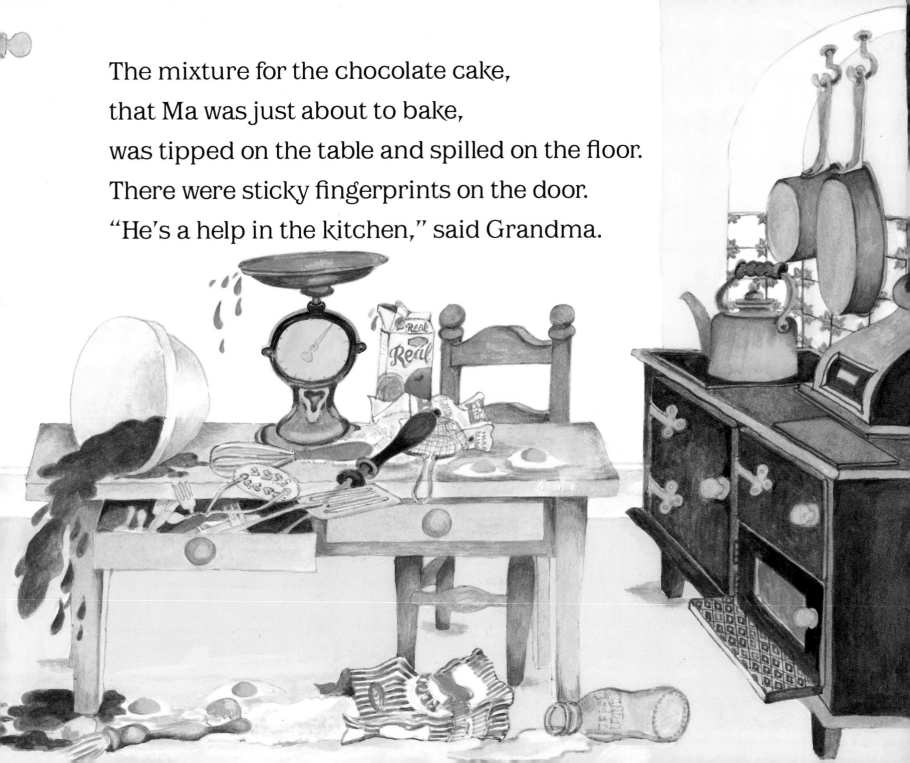

They followed the fingerprints on the wall
towards Pa's workroom in the hall.

Hazel opened the door and they all peered in.
"How clever!" said Grandma, "he's opened a tin!"
Paint trickled and dripped all over Pa's tools,
and lay on the floor in glossy pools.
"He's taken a brush," said Hazel.

The wall from the workroom was striped in red.
"It stops at the living room," Hazel said.
"He's good at painting," said Grandma.

"What a help!" Grandma said. "What a lot he can do.
He's been cleaning the living room chimney for you!"
The new white carpet was not so white,
and fingerprints as black as night
covered the sofa and both the chairs,
circled the walls —

then went upstairs.

"He's a good little climber," said Grandma.

They followed Hazel
who raced ahead,

into the bathroom the fingerprints led.

"What a memory!" said Grandma.
"He must have been told
not to touch the hot tap.
He's turned on the cold."
Talcum powder was thick on the floor,
and little white footprints went out of the door.

Ma and Pa's bedroom door was ajar.
"I'm sure I closed it this morning," said Ma.
"He must have opened it on his own,
I keep forgetting how much he's grown!"
"He's tall for his age," said Grandma.

The dress Ma was making was shorter than planned.
"He can use scissors," said Grandma. "Isn't that grand!"
The scarf Ma was knitting for Uncle Fred
had been unravelled all over the bed.
Wool wiggled and curved across the floor,
and they followed the wiggles out of the door.

"Oh dear," said Ma, "where can he be?"

"Don't worry," said Grandma cheerfully.

"I'm sure that we will find him soon.

He's probably tidying Hazel's room."

All Hazel's books had been pulled from the shelf.

"He must have been trying to read them himself,"
said Grandma, "and look how he tried to write on the wall.
It's hard to believe he's a baby at all!"

There was one room left....

So they tiptoed in. A tiny room as neat as a pin.

Not a toy out of place or a mark on the wall.

"He can't have been in here at all,"

said Ma. "It's far too clean."

But she hadn't seen what Hazel had seen.

"Oh!" cried Grandma, "isn't he sweet!"

"Yes," said Hazel, "when he's asleep."

"He does sleep soundly,"
said Grandma.